Tales from the CANYONS of the DAMNED

PRESENTED BY USA TODAY BESTSELLING AUTHOR
DANIEL ARTHUR SMITH

Tales from the Canyons of the Damned 31

Collection Copyright © 2019 by Daniel Arthur Smith

Fortune Cookies by Hunter C. Eden. Copyright © 2019 Hunter C. Eden. Used by permission of the author.

That Time of Year by D.K. Cassidy. Copyright © 2019 D.K. Cassidy. Used by permission of the author.

The Pairing Witch by David Alan Jones. Copyright © 2019 David Alan Jones. Used by permission of the author.

Similar by Holly Heisey. Copyright © 2018 Holly Heisey. Used by permission of the author.

#Eddie_and_June by Daniel Arthur Smith. Copyright © 2019 Daniel Arthur Smith. Used by permission of the author.

First Edition

Special thanks to editor Jessica West

ISBN: 978-1-946777-80-5

Cover By Daniel Arthur Smith

Horror Fiction from Holt Smith ltd
Agroland
Tower
Attack of the Kung Fu Mummies

For Susan, Tristan, & Oliver, as all things are.

Fortune Cookies
Hunter C. Eden

THANK YOU FOR CALLING Great Wall Foods of America. Regrettably, we have no service representatives available. Please leave a message and a service representative will get back to you as soon as possible.

This is Shirley Lynner and I'm calling because my son always gets (pardon my French) the shittiest fortunes with his cookies. I started saving them after awhile, and I have some of them right here. "You would do well to avoid greed." He's eight. Show me an eight-year old who isn't greedy. "Desire is the enemy of harmony." Look, I don't appreciate having my son preached to by Confucianists. He can desire whatever he wants. "You are learned in the ways of love." Jesus, he's eight years old! We've explained to him what happens between mommies and daddies, but that doesn't mean he's learned in the ways of love, and I don't want him trying to be. "The stars will remain above, and man below them." "Hell's fires are breezes to those of the heart." "Restore the Qing, destroy the foreigner."

1

What kinds of fortunes are these to give to an eight-year-old boy? I'm no Buddha, but do you know what I think are good fortunes? "You're very good at sports." "People like you." "You're really smart." Those are good fortunes.

Call me back, because I want to discuss this with someone. You can reach me at (410) 555-7965.

Hello, you have reached the voice-mail box of Shirley Lynner. I'm not here right now, but leave a message and I will get back to you as soon as possible.

Hello, Mrs. Lynner, this is Zhang with Great Wall Foods of America returning your call. Technically speaking, none of the notes you read over the phone, or even your suggestions, are what I would call fortunes. A fortune is a prediction of the future, generally obtained by some magical practice. During the Shang Dynasty, for instance, applying heated irons to the scapulae of animals produced series of cracks that could be used to divine the future. Of course, the size of a scapula, not to mention the cost of cracking by heated iron rod, precludes us from baking an actual divinatory bone into a cookie. In addition, these scapulae can't just be read by you and me, but require a professional fortuneteller or shaman to be properly interpreted. Such individuals are rare, and employing even one at a corner Chinese eatery would make it almost impossible for the restaurant to achieve budget. But, of course, we have to market them as "fortune" cookies because that's the name the market has given us.

As for your son's unsatisfactory cookie notes, I want to assure you that we have a number of talented and trained writers on hand laboring their hardest to provide only the highest quality messages in your cookies. We urge you to go back to the restaurant where you purchased them and try again. After all, random chance ensures that eventually a good and relevant cookie will appear with your check. In the meantime, please accept a free box of Great Wall Foods fortune cookies and a sincere apology on the part of the executive and writing staff. May we have your address?

Thank you for calling Great Wall Foods, and we hope we have solved your problem.

Thank you for calling Great Wall Foods of America. Regrettably, we have no service representatives available. Please leave a message and a service representative will get back to you as soon as possible.

Hello, Zhang? This is Shirley Lynner again—I'm the one who complained about the fortunes. I want you to know that I don't need to be told what is and isn't a fortune, particularly by a company that seems completely and totally incapable of writing them.

I'd like to accept your offer of cookies, but I want you to know that my son will be eating those cookies only under my or my husband's supervision until we deem your fortunes constructive and appropriate for an eight-year old reader.

You can send the cookies to 336 Arbor Lane, Columbia, Maryland, 21046.

Hello, you've reached the voice-mail box of Shirley Lynner. I'm not here right now, but leave a message and I will get back to you as soon as possible.

Mrs. Lynner, this is Zhang with Great Wall Foods of America. We will send the box of cookies out to you as soon as possible. We apologize again for any difficulty we have caused you.

Thank you for calling Great Wall Foods of America. Regrettably, we have no service representatives available. Please leave a message and a service representative will get back to you as soon as possible.

This is Shirley Lynner, and I'm calling to tell you that my husband and I will never buy any Great Wall Foods products again, and I'll tell all my friends just what kind of service you've given us. My husband and I opened a few of the cookies just to make sure they had content suitable for our son. Do you know what my first fortune said? "You will die happily in the arms of a lover." You're running a disgusting business, Zhang or whoever you are, and my husband and I aren't going to support it or be threatened by it.

Hello, you've reached the voice-mail box of Shirley Lynner. I'm not here right now, but leave a message and I will get back to you as soon as possible.

Mrs. Lynner, it saddens me to hear of your dissatisfaction with our product here at Great Wall Foods of America. The fortune you referenced was quite an educational one, but I'd like to speak with you in person if possible to clear up this difficulty and explain it better. Our factory is located at 39 Willow Street, Gaithersburg. We are open twenty-four hours a day, so just call before you come, and we will make all the proper preparations.

Thank you for calling Great Wall Foods of America. Regrettably, we have no service representatives available. Please leave a message and a service representative will get back to you as soon as possible.

Shirley Lynner here. It's two p.m. and I'm coming down to your factory now. I just want you to know that I've called my husband and a couple friends of ours, and if I don't call them in three hours, the police will be alerted.

You've reached the answering service of Jim Lynner. I'm busy with a client at the moment, but if you leave a message I will return your call as promptly as possible.

Dad? It's me, Shawn. Do you know where Mom is? Andy's dad had to give me a ride home from soccer practice.

Hello, you've reached the voice-mail box of Shirley Lynner. I'm not here right now, but leave a message and I will get back to you as soon as possible.

Sweetie, it's Jim. I don't know where you are, but—

Everything's okay, honey. The tour just went a little long.

You took a tour? I thought you were complaining about the cookies.

It started that way, but Mr. Zhang filled me in on their company policy, and then as a courtesy he gave me a tour and explained a little bit about Chinese culture.

Are you okay, Shirl'? You sound worn out.

I had a very long, hard day, Jim.

Thank you for calling Great Wall Foods of America. Regrettably, we have no service representatives available. Please leave a message and a service representative will get back to you as soon as possible.

Mr. Zhang? It's me, Shirley Lynner. You told me you were the First Emperor, that you'd lived for two thousand years and you'd learned so much you wanted to show me. You said you made yourself immortal by devouring the pleasure of women, using their *chi* to lengthen your life. I'm guessing you're telling the truth.

You Taoist tease. I want another tour, and I have no more complaints.

Hello, you've reached the voice-mail box of Shirley Lynner. I'm not here right now, but leave a message and I will get back to you as soon as possible.

Mrs. Lynner? Mr. Zhang. I regret having used such a simplistic, ridiculous line, but when faced with your affronted beauty, I found I could not think of anything more fitting. I wanted you, Mrs. Lynner, more than I've wanted anyone in two millennia. Come for your tour whenever you want.

Hello, you've reached the voice-mail box of Shirley Lynner. I'm not here right now, but leave a message and I will get back to you as soon as possible.

Mom? It's me, Shawn. I was wondering where—

I'm busy right now, Shawn. There's a frozen chicken nugget dinner in the freezer.

What do I put on the microwave for that?

One three oh, defrost, start. I'll talk to you later, Shawn.

Are you at the gym? You sound like you've been running.

I'll talk to you later, Shawn.

This is the Goldstein Medical Associates automated mailbox. If you know your party's extension, dial it now. If not, stay on the line and an operator will assist you.

Five, seven, five, three.

This is Dr. Richard Goldstein. I'll be out until next Monday. Please leave a message after the tone. If this is an emergency, hang up and dial 911.

Hello, Dr. Goldstein, this is Jim Lynner and I'm calling about my wife, Shirley. Basically, she's not really eating much, and she's been losing a lot of weight over the past five weeks. I don't know if this would be like an eating

It never takes long to convince a man to go home with her.

His name is Jason. She hasn't had a Jason before.

He leaves behind his half-finished drink and climbs up the stairs, eyes focused on Delilah's face, wrapped in a trance of lust and curiosity.

The doorman to the building nods to Delilah. He rarely sees her, but when he does, her sultry beauty delights him. He watches her walk hand-in-hand with a good-looking man on their way to the elevator leading to her penthouse. The golden doors open, and they walk in. As the doors close, he has a last glimpse of the couple. He knows he won't be seeing that man again.

As they enter her apartment, she lets go of Jason's hand and motions for him to stop. Delilah goes to the kitchen, opens up the refrigerator, and pulls out a bottle of her favorite champagne. Two crystal flutes on her marble counter wait for her to fill them. She pours a full glass for him and half a glass for herself. She looks into the living room to be sure he hasn't moved.

Then, she opens her ring and takes out a small tablet, discreetly depositing it into his glass. It fizzes, but so does the champagne, so it won't be noticeable. She brings out the flutes and encircles her arm with his as they drink the bubbly, staring into one another's eyes.

Glasses drained, he asks, "What's your name? You never told me back at the Palm Court."

No answer from Delilah. Instead, she takes his hand and leads him into her bedroom. He doesn't seem bothered by her lack of response. He smiles in anticipation of what is to come.

Her king-sized bed is decorated with a red cover and two large velvet pillows. Each poster on her bed has a long black cord tied to it.

Jason smiles and asks her if she's kinky. Again, Delilah doesn't answer. She points to the bed and unzips her dress.

In a rush, he unbuttons his shirt and pulls off his pants. As he begins to take off his boxers, Delilah shakes her head. She motions to the bed. Jason lays down and watches as she ties his arms and legs to the posts. He turns his head to the right and looks puzzled.

"What are these scratches on the bedpost?"

For the first time since they entered her apartment, Delilah speaks.

"I'm keeping track. Now lay back and enjoy the evening."

The clock in the next room strikes midnight. Delilah pulls her ancient knife from under one of the large pillows.

She shuts the door to her bedroom, reliving the events of the night. Next year will bring her collection to one hundred.

Time to move to another city, she thinks. She's been here for twenty years, never aging. Delilah knows her neighbors are suspicious.

The ancient atlas in her living room sits on its pedestal, cloaked in a light layer of dust. It hasn't been touched for a year. She grabs it then throws it in the air while whispering the magical words. It lands upside down. Turning it over, she finds her next home. New Orleans.

Delilah hasn't been there for eighty years. Anyone who knew her then would be dead or demented. She won't be recognized. A rare smile spreads on her face; this city is one of her favorites.

Delilah blows a kiss in the direction of Jason. In her right hand is her smartphone, filled with photos of him, and all of her other men. Or rather, images of their hearts. Always in the same position on her bed. The heart is placed with loving care next to their silent bodies.

"Time to buy a new mattress", she says to the empty room. Her black cat circles her leg, purring her approval.

The Pairing Witch
David Alan Jones

"YOU'RE NOTHING LIKE I expected a witch to be." Princess Neorah Vannul, her glossy blond locks gleaming in the afternoon sun, leaned out the carriage window on one delicate elbow to peer at the woman keeping pace with her.

"What did you expect?" Della couldn't suppress a smile.

"I don't know. Someone old I suppose. How old are you, Della?"

"Neorah," said Queen Beatrice from somewhere within the padded confines of the carriage. "What a thing to say to another woman."

"She's not a woman, Mother, she's a witch. Did I offend you, Della?"

"No, Highness."

"See, Mother?" Neorah turned back to Della, one eyebrow raised.

"I'm twenty-six, your Highness."

Neorah's mouth dropped open, her pretty red lips forming a perfect O. "Are you really? I never would have guessed. You look hardly older than me. Why aren't you married?"

Della felt her cheeks grow hot.

"And now I have embarrassed you." The princess pursed her lips, looking pensive. "I am sorry. Truly. It's just, I'm so nervous."

"I know, your Highness."

"Della, do stop the highnesses. I thought I broke you of that on the second day of this horrid journey. Did you see the Locke earlier?"

"I did, Your High—yes, I did."

"It's a rather small castle, isn't it?" Neorah gazed at the near line of forest only a few hundred feet from the muddy road as if she might peer through them.

"We are some miles off," Della said. "And we've only glimpsed it through the trees. Perhaps it will seem larger as we draw nearer."

"You're sweet, but I know I'm bringing far more to this marriage than the prince."

"You're keeping your crown and your personal fortune," said the queen's muffled voice from inside.

"Mother, please. I'm trying to have a conversation here," Neorah said over one shoulder. Then to Della, she said, "What do you think he's really like? He can't be the tyrant they claim, can he?"

"Perhaps he's merely boorish—not one for society."

"And what of his looks? He's just twenty-one, not even five years my senior, but they say he's hideous."

"You know rumors, my Lady," Della said, glancing down at a hangnail. "They blow like clouds and change shape twice as fast. Probably the man has a cowlick is all."

Neorah laughed. "A cowlick? Reminds me of what my old nan used to say, 'Trust a pairing witch when it comes to love, but plug your ears when it comes to men.'"

"A wise woman," Della said, grinning back.

"We are friends, aren't we, Della?"

Though she never would have credited it two weeks before, Della found herself nodding. "You know we are, your High—my Lady."

Neorah nodded slowly and leaned forward to whisper, "I never asked you about the magic did I? Not once this whole way."

"No. You didn't," Della whispered back.

"Will you tell me what it's like? What happens at the pairing?"

"You know I cannot, Highness."

"You're going to do this thing to me—to my betrothed—can I not know how it feels beforehand?"

Della pushed a coal-black strand of hair from her eyes to glance at the princess. Young though she was, Neorah had a way about her, a logical method of thinking and talking that could woo a worm from an apple core. "This is my first pairing without a mentor watching my work. I must do well here, or return to Coven House in shame."

"I'm being cruel, aren't I? Break no oaths on my behalf. I withdraw the question."

"No," Della said. "I want to tell you. You've been kind to me, far more so than I deserve. I've never had a real person for a friend, much less a princess."

"Real person? Now you've intrigued me. Whatever does that mean?"

Della's cheeks grew hot. "I'm so sorry, my Lady. It—it's what we at Coven House call people without magic. It means those without the burden of magic."

"Are there none but witches there?"

Della nodded.

"Is it because of the hate?" Neorah asked.

Della almost stumbled. "You know of that?"

"Some." Neorah looked supremely satisfied at surprising the witch. "I know that your magic makes people hate you."

Slowly, Della nodded. "Have you ever heard the principle of parchment, my Lady?"

"No."

"It is a way of understanding the Wending Way without knowing its craft. Shall I tell it to you?"

"Please."

"Imagine a square of parchment. Picture hands rolling it into a funnel, holding it that way for just a moment, and then releasing it to unfurl into its original shape. Do you see it, my Lady?"

"I do."

"Thus a witch controls another's mind. But doing so breeds enmity with those around her."

"Because of what you've done to them?"

"No, because I use a bit of my soul every time I cast. Non-casters sense this without realizing it, and they cannot but hate one so diminished. They go on hating us until our souls grow back."

"You can grow back your soul?" Neorah had the air of a woman who has just learned her bosom companion can flap her arms and fly around the twin moons.

"Unless I cause it a severe injury, yes."

"But I thought your spells were permanent. Won't Prince Trevard and I love one another our whole lives? Will our attachment for one another unfurl like rolled parchment? I should not enjoy one day waking next to a man I loathe."

"Yes, my Lady, the pairing shall be permanent. That is the second principle of parchment. We call it folding. If you fold parchment it will remain folded. Even if you unfold it, the paper will never be the same again. That is pairing. I fold your mind, just as I will fold the prince's, creating a permanent change of heart."

Neorah chewed on that for a moment, her eyes downcast. Then she looked up, her brow furrowed with sudden worry. "Is the hate also permanent?"

"In the case of folding, yes, it is because the effect is permanent."

"What of the other witches? Do they hate you? How has Coven House stood for all these centuries if the witches and warlocks despise one another?"

"Those who can touch the Wending Way are immune to the effect."

"Am I going to hate you after tonight?" Neorah looked pained.

"Yes, my Lady. I'm afraid you will. Always."

The carriage swung into a narrow lane before the castle's main entrance where waited no fewer than fifty servants dressed in the silver and purple livery of House Locke. Della watched from behind a good-sized hedgerow off to one side of the proceedings. Weeks of travel had left their mark on her dress and boots. She would have a bath and change into clean robes for the ceremony tonight. In the meantime, should Neorah demand it, she would certainly present herself, but she figured the princess had other things on her mind just now besides a muddied pairing witch.

A trumpeter blatted a fanfare from an overhead balcony, and a middle-aged butler hurried to open the carriage door with a squire in tow to place a step for its occupants.

At the same time, a young man dressed in fine, pearl white silk strung together with silver thread descended from the castle's entryway. He was followed by an elderly couple, each of them dressed as lavishly as he with golden coronets encircling their brows.

Could that man be the prince of rumor? Hidden behind the hedge's foilage, Della goggled. The young man, who by the look of him was closer to her own age than Neorah's, stood tall, back erect, dark hair cascading to his shoulders. Broad of chest and slim of hip, he moved with exquisite grace like a seasoned dancer or blade master.

Queen Beatrice exited the carriage, leaning heavily on the butler's proffered hand.

"Her Highness, Queen Beatrice of Vale," said the lead steward who stood at the head of the Locke's gathered servants, his baritone carrying throughout the square.

Neorah flounced from the carriage after her mother, adroit as a young doe, her maids struggling to keep pace. As she landed, her bell-shaped skirts billowed prettily like a cloud of gold and lavender. An appreciative murmur rose from the gathered commoners and servants alike.

"Her Highness, Princess Neorah of Vale." The steward raised his voice even higher than he had for Queen Beatrice.

"Welcome to our home." King Thomasard Blaylocke bowed to the silken ladies. "This is my wife, Queen Faya, and of course, our son, Prince Trevard."

The prince smiled, and Della thought her breast might collapse in on itself for his comeliness. Though no one stood nearby to see, a warm flush of embarrassment ran hot up her neck and into her cheeks. If it was embarrassment.

"It is a pleasure to meet you at last, my Prince." Neorah bowed as she would to a peer, her demure lips curved upward in a pleased smile.

And well you should smile, Della thought, trying in vain to quell the thorn of envy twisting in her navel.

The prince returned Neorah's bow in kind. He too looked pleased at what he saw.

"Won't you join us inside for some refreshment?" King Thomasar took his lady wife's arm to guide her up the steps.

"Indeed." Queen Beatrice started to follow, the butler still bearing the brunt of her not inconsiderable weight.

"Aren't you going to welcome me to the Locke?" Neorah stared pointedly at the prince, one eyebrow raised. "You can't imagine the lengths we've gone to keeping this dress presentable on the road."

"You do look lovely, dear," Queen Faya said, looking back. "But you must be simply exhausted. Do come inside."

"Doesn't he talk?" Neorah asked.

Queen Faya giggled, her eyes roving from her husband to her son several times before finally settling on Queen Beatrice. She put on a faux smile, her eyes rueful. "Of course he does. What a question."

"Honestly, Neorah. You embarrass us. Come along," said her mother.

"No." Neorah crossed her arms.

"What did she say?" King Thomasar asked.

"I said no. I'm not moving until my betrothed properly welcomes me to my new home."

"Neorah!" Queen Beatrice's face paled in the darkling light.

The princess squared herself with the prince, and though she was two hands shorter than the man, it was he who shrank back. "I have traveled three hundred miles to reach this place. My people crossed the Balanth's Blade in high melt. We lost three horses and a drover. I slept, ate, and groomed in that horrid carriage for days. And yet mine is the greater kingdom by three times. The least you could say is, 'Welcome to Denholm, Princess Neorah.'"

Thick silence fell. Even the sound of servants unloading carts in the stables seemed suddenly muted. The prince, eyes round with either effrontery or fear, looked to his mother and father. Queen Faya's face fell when the king gave his son a brief, pained nod.

"Welcome to Denholm, Princess Neorah," Prince Trevard said.

One of the servants, Della thought it might have been the head butler, groaned, and several others gasped. Queen Faya glared at her son with unmistakable rage, while the king drew back a step as if he'd been struck in the face.

Neorah let go a little moo of displeasure, one hand flying to her breast, the other held out as if to ward off the prince.

A look of such pain and remorse crossed Prince Trevard's face in that moment that Della could not but love him. No one but she saw the black ribbon which had issued from his mouth when he spoke. It jiggled and curved, bending to touch nearly every person standing near him. As it did, those touched turned their gazes to the prince, their expressions darkening with anger, even hatred.

"How dare you speak to my daughter that way!" Queen Beatrice, her hands balled into fists at her sides, looked ready to do battle with outrage alone.

"He doesn't mean it," Queen Faya said. "He never says the right thing."

Della had heard—had seen—enough. She strode forward, muddy skirts flapping. "Stop!"

All eyes turned to her as a ribbon spewed from her own lips to touch every person within earshot. "I am the pairing witch, Della. I have been contracted to match these two. Escort us to a private room for the ceremony. Now!"

It took several minutes to sort out just who should find a room for the witch and her couple, since two queens and a king seemed bent on outrunning fifty servants to the task. But inside a quarter hour, Della found herself standing in King Thomasar's solar, Neorah seated by one wall and Prince Trevard sulking by the other.

"I should like—" Della began, but Neorah spoke over her.

"I will not marry this man. I'd rather lose Vale and all my holdings."

Trevard winced and opened his mouth to speak.

"No." Della held up a hand to forestall him. "Please, your Highness, I beg of you, not a word."

"It doesn't matter what you say, Della. My decision is made." Neorah glared at the prince with vile enmity.

Della knelt before her friend, and though she worried she might overstep her station, she took Neorah's hands. "You do not hate him."

"I do."

"No. You react to him, because he is a Warlock."

Neorah's eyes went round. She glanced at the prince then back to Della. "He's like you?"

Della nodded.

"That doesn't excuse the things he said."

"What did he say? Do you remember anything untoward?"

Neorah shifted uncomfortably in her chair. She could not meet Della's eyes.

"You can think of none, because he said only kind words to you." Della squeezed the princess's hands.

"You can't see it, because you aren't royal."

"No. I'm unaffected because I do see it."

"What was that?" The prince tilted his head to one side, his green eyes narrowed. "You see what?"

Neorah's eyes bulged and she bared her teeth in a snarl of feral anger. "How dare you speak to Della like that?" The princess made to rise, but Della forced her back.

"Sit," the witch said, a black ribbon gushing from her lips like smoke. It touched Neorah's forehead and the princess immediately ceased struggling. "Sleep." A pang of remorse stabbed at Della's heart for so coarsely using the other woman, but there was nothing for it. Neorah's eyes rolled back and she fell limp.

"What have you done?" Trevard hurried forward as if he might part the witch from his betrothed.

"Calm yourself, my Prince. She sleeps."

"What is that coming from your lips?" Trevard stumbled to a stop, his eyes grown wide.

"A streamer of soul," Della said. "The same as yours. You've seen it issue from your own mouth a thousand times, I'd wager."

The prince gazed at her in wonder. "You aren't angry at hearing my voice?"

Della shook her head.

"Why?"

"We are alike, my Lord. We of Wend and Way."

"But the princess, she cannot see our—our magic?"

"No."

The prince watched the sleeping princess for a long moment. When finally he lifted his gaze back to regard Della, his expression burned with desire. "Marry me."

"What?" Della nearly stumbled over Neorah's chair so great was her surprise.

"You are the first woman I've ever met who could stand to hear more than three words from my mouth. Do you know how long I've craved just this modicum of intimacy? I would make you my queen just to gain your ear."

Della was shaking. Her heart must surely be bruising itself against her breastbone. "You could love me?"

"I would love you, Lady, as no man has ever loved another." Trevard stretched a trembling hand out to her, his expression anxious and fearful. How many times had he reached out for another's touch in just this manner and received only scorn even from his own kin?

Almost, she took his hand. Almost, Della forgot her duty. But no. He was not for her. What had she to offer him but solace? Neorah had the crown. Neorah had the armies and the lush crop lands and the titles that would pass to their progeny. She had the proper claim on this man. The unification of their houses would bring peace and prosperity to both their kingdoms.

What did Della have to rival that? Nothing but her magic.

"I cannot," she said.

"I want no other." Though Trevard dropped his hand, his eyes remained on her, imploring. "Am I to live my life a mute, unable even to address my wife, my children, my servants for fear of turning their souls against me?"

"No." Della steeled herself for what she must do, realizing in that moment it would take all of her might.

She had heard of the Cleansing before—the ritual meant to scour another's soul clean of Wend and Way—though she had never seen it performed. And yet, she knew she could do it the way she knew she could draw breath. "You shall not. I will take this burden from you, Prince, though it will require my very life."

Della drew from within herself such a torrent of soul, its passage set her insides on fire. A ribbon thick as her wrist shot from her lips, and she screamed. The ribbon split and split again until it ran like a great river whose tributaries encompassed the globe, and still it flowed on and on, each of its smoking fingers bending to touch the prince here and here and here until it covered his body in a gyrating miasma of greasy smoke.

Still, the magic demanded more. Della poured out all she could reach. Then she reached again. Blood leaked from her nose, the corners of her mouth, her eyes and her ears. Still she reached, still she drew, for though she had never folded another witch, she somehow sensed doing so would require all of her.

Princess Neorah awoke in a chair. Her mouth tasted like cat droppings, and her legs were stiff.

She rose, momentarily disoriented, until she recognized the king's solar by the light of breaking dawn streaming through the room's stained glass windows.

Prince Trevard lay on a narrow divan at the center of the room, his chest rising and falling in deep slumber. At sight of his face, a warm flush of yearning rushed through Neorah's breast. And though the feeling confused her, she nevertheless trusted its ardor.

"My prince." She gave Trevard a gentle shake.

His green eyes fluttered open and he sat up with a start. "The witch, Della. Where has she gone?"

Neorah frowned. Why was he asking after Della? A thoughtless dart of rage and hatred singed her heart at mention of the meddlesome witch, but Neorah's love seemed genuinely concerned for the woman, so she spun in a slow circle. "Della isn't—" Neorah froze.

Muddied boots, too small to fit a man, jutted out from one side of the couch. Neorah screamed.

Della lay on her back, desiccated eyes watching the ceiling, face pale as milk, no life in it. Rivulets of dried blood painted her pallid cheeks.

"What has happened to her?" Trevard asked.

Neorah could not answer. No words would pass the rock in her throat. For though the witch kindled within her a smoldering anger, she experienced a sudden stab of loss as if someone she loved had passed from this mortal life. She turned and buried herself in the prince's arms. At first, he tensed, standing awkwardly, but slowly he relaxed, his arms reaching to complete their embrace.

"You heard my voice and yet you hold me?" Trevard tightened his grip on Neorah who snuggled closer to him, her hot tears wet on his neck.

"Why do you sound so surprised, my Prince?" Neorah pulled back to gaze into Trevard's green eyes. "I love you."

For a moment, he only stared at her, confusion warring with elation across the battlefield of his face. At last, he favored her with a timid smile, one she would only grow to love all the more as the years of their lives together wore on. "And I you, my love."

Similar

Holly Heisey

Day 3. Now.

WHEN THE THING APPEARED in my living room, my husband fled, yelling, "Matt, what the hell did you do?"

It's like a modern art sculpture, all black sinew and sinister edges. I've seen enough of Brent's gallery showings to know. It's growing from floor to ceiling, but I checked and it's not in the basement or the upstairs bedroom.

There's a blackbird, too, which appeared on my bookshelf. I didn't notice it the first day, it blends with the ebony of the shelf. But on the second day, it stirred.

Okay, I can't keep calling it the Thing. That's too bad-horror-movie. It is the Sculpture in Matt's Living Room. SIMLR.

Today I got up the courage to touch the SIMLR. It's warm and pulses like it's breathing. The breath is labored.

Day -634. Before.

I met Brent in a gallery. Of course it was a gallery, with violent pink canvasses on white walls, chrome monstrosities spread in a forest across the floor, and spray-painted beer cans hanging artfully from the ceiling. And among all the chaos was beautiful darkness. Matte-black pillars growing up like fluid stalagmites. Geometric, fractal, moving me when I thought all this stuff was junk and all I really wanted to do was go home and delve into my books and I was only at the gallery because I owed a friend a night's wingmanship.

Then I looked up from his art and saw him. Tall. Neatly-trimmed hipster beard. Black-rimmed glasses and the cutest shy dimple when he smiled.

There are moments in life when your reality shifts. A quantum tipping point from one state to another. An observation that changes your state from one to two.

Day 4. Now.

The blackbird woke up. It sits on a stack of physics books and tilts its head when I mutter to myself, listening.

The SIMLR's curves don't ever quite look the same, like it's edging forward in glacial motion. It's not geometrical and rigid like Brent's sculptures, but built as if for movement. I think it's heading toward the front door. Does it want out?

I can't look away.

Day -332. Before.

I never thought I'd go for marriage. I'd never wanted a boyfriend, much less a husband. Working shifts as a manager at an electronics store and a second job as a cashier at a geek shop kept me more than busy. Brent said I was wasted on those jobs. I should have gone to college and studied physics, which was what I spent most of my spare time reading about. My real passion, outside of Brent. Physics and metaphysics, but Brent wasn't so sure about the metaphysics. "Fake science," he called it.

Brent didn't get that the brown suit, red bowtie, and fez (which he talked me out of) I wore on our wedding day was an homage to my favorite British science fiction show. Brent thought science fiction was nonsense.

"Why waste your time on things that aren't real when you can be changing the universe, love?"

I brushed brown hair out of his eyes. "You spend all day creating matte black variations on a theme. Isn't that making things that aren't real? They're gorgeous, yes. But not real."

"Art is real. Art is tangible. Art anchors us to reality."

Does it?

Day 6. Now.

I read a lot. Brent says I should be searching for another job—or jobs—but he doesn't know how hard it is out there. The doors to his studio in town, in which he's been sleeping the last few nights, and the doors to the galleries where he shows, are like portals. There's a different reality on the other side of those doors than the one I live in out here.

So I read about M-theory and quantum mechanics, about multiverses and other dimensions, the nature of thoughts and reality. I'd seriously like to change mine.

The blackbird keeps watching me, so I explain my theories, how maybe we think about something and it changes on the quantum level. Not just the state shifts in particles when they're observed, but actual, tangible reality. Thoughts driving the nature of reality. I really want this to be true.

The blackbird says, "Hello, Matt."

I peed myself when it spoke. I just toweled off before I wrote this down. I need a shower.

Also, the SIMLR is three feet closer to my door than the first day.

Day 8. Now.

Brent called. He's not coming back from the city until I take care of our vermin problem.

"Matt, I didn't make that thing. I don't care if you said it looks like something I'd make—it's obscene. And I know you didn't make it. You just don't have the imagination for that. So that's too weird for me, okay? That's just too weird. You're…"

I don't have the imagination for that? I stiffen, every muscle inside me growing silent.

There's a pause, and I hear him breathing on the other side of the phone. It's a pause like the moment before sleep. The death of a day.

"Matt, I love you, okay?" It's like he's testing the words.

And I'm testing hearing them.

"Okay," I say.

He doesn't say that I have issues. But I know he's thinking it. I hear it in the soft beep as he hangs up.

The blackbird sits on its stack of books and hums to itself. It never flies. Its head droops, and it jerks it up with a chirp.

"If you're that tired, just sleep," I snap.

"Oh, no. If I sleep, I will cease to exist."

"What? Why?"

That moment before sleep. The death of a day.

It fixes me with a cock-eyed stare. Its stare shifts the air from my concern to his. "Leave."

The hairs on my arms rise. Neither the blackbird nor the SIMLR has tried to get me to do anything before now. This feels momentous, and I don't think I like it.

"I can't leave." The SIMLR hasn't hurt me. I'm not unsafe, am I?

I look at the SIMLR, its shimmering strangeness.

This is my home. Maybe Brent's not in it right now, and maybe the home feels empty without him. But...it's still my home.

"I can't leave," I say again, softly.

The blackbird nods sagely as if I've said something wise, then goes back to trying not to fall asleep.

Day -109. Before.

"I don't want kids, okay?" Brent shoved his sketch pad away. We were sitting at the dining room table in our new home, boxes still scattered around us. Not boxes with Brent's sculptures, though. He always wanted to keep his art separate, in his studio, in the sterile, too-bright worlds of his galleries. Even though I loved his work, and even though when we were both near it we felt a deeper connection than when we weren't. I haven't figured that correlation out yet.

I studied my hands, palms on the table. I was tired. Moving was hard, and I'd just started my latest job as a manager at an office supply store. It was hardly different than my last job as a manager at a sporty clothing store. It was a job.

"I want more than this," I started to say, but Brent cut a hand through the air.

"Isn't that what this house is for? So we can have a permanent place together, not just a series of random apartments? God, Matt. We just moved in. The extra bedroom's for an office, not a nursery. I don't want kids."

We'd discussed this before. And I'd tried to tell him I wanted my life to mean something more than it did. And that meaning had nothing to do with if I was happy being with him or not—I loved him. I loved him, and if I wanted to raise children with anyone, I wanted it to be him. I wanted us to raise a kid, or two, or three, the sums of both of us. I wanted to learn how the reality of my life would merge with his and create something new. Both our talents inherent in our children. New realities, utterly new creations.

"It's too expensive," Brent said. "Adoption's just—it's too expensive. And what will people think? I mean, we still get looks, and we're legally married. It's stupid. But I hate it. But to have kids? I'm not even good with kids. You know that, Matt."

It was probably true. I'd seen him not even look at kids when they approached him in his gallery showings. He didn't know what to do with them.

But he'd been home less and less lately, consumed by his work. Or possibly less consumed with me. I'd thought buying a house together would give a sense of permanence, but the threads of the walls were unraveling. Raising a child would be something we could do together. Help us recombine. We really had to get out on more dates, because the times at night I wanted to binge space shows and he wanted to sketch quietly—the two states not mutually compatible—were adding up.

I wanted a child. Something for me. A dull ache in a growing collection of needs that I kept shoving under the bed and trying to ignore.

Day 9. Now.

The blackbird stares at me with fatigue-dulled eyes. It mutters, "Leave, leave, leave."

Doesn't it see that I can't? The SIMLR is not supposed to be here. It's not from this reality. But when I look at it, I feel safer than when I look away. Maybe that should scare me.

It is almost to the door.

Day 1. Beginning.

Brent says that when he doesn't create, he feels like death is right beside him. Waiting to take him. He pours his life and his soul into his sculptures so that he can keep breathing.

I've thought about this for a long time. I don't have a talent like Brent's. I can't take iron or stone and make it submit. My reality is less tangible, full of things that have begun to lose their glamor for me.

My reality is colder, full of a person who has cooled in my heart.

My reality is physics I barely understand, and thoughts I wish to be true. But it is my reality. And if I'm to find anything more than death waiting to take me, I have to pour my life and soul into something, too.

So I take everything I know. Everything I've learned. Everything about multiple dimensions and malleable realities and quantum states. My life has been set to off, and I need it back on again. I close my eyes and pour my life and my soul into a reality I can handle.

When I open my eyes, the SIMLR is there.

Day 9. Now.

When I look at the SIMLR, I think about Brent. Brent is dark and sinewy and alien to me. We live together, but we never expand beyond our own borders.

The SIMLR is turning towards me as I write.

The blackbird was almost asleep, but now it's waking.

I've been playing with changing realities. If the SIMLR is from another reality, a reality I need, what does that mean? What does it mean that it looks like what I remember of that first night I saw Brent among his matte black pillars? But when I see pictures of those sculptures from that night, they look wrong to me. Different. As if the reality they came from has shifted away. They used to be my anchors, but now they're as adrift as I am.

I'm trapped in this room where I spend my time. I can't get another job. Not now. The world outside is too open, the reality of that world and my world and Brent's world too disparate—but I can't leave Brent. Even apart, our selves are so entangled I don't know enough of myself outside the context of him. When he is here, though, it's like I'm falling asleep. I'm losing myself. That small moment before the death of a day.

I tilt my head and study the SIMLR. It feels fresh somehow, like I'm seeing it for the first time. Or maybe it's changed since I called it from its reality.

It's how I see myself, isn't it? Strange and wrong. But in motion. Moving slowly toward the door.

It's how I see Brent. It's how he needs to leave, and how I need to leave, how we are both drowning in the strangeness of each other. And I am the blackbird, too fatigued to fly.

The SIMLR shifts from black to granite to stone. It pulls down from the borders of the ceiling and opens a portal lined up with the front door. The blackbird leaps from the stack of books and soars through, and through the glass window beside the door. It flies free outside.

When I walk through the portal, I know the SIMLR will be gone. I will no longer need its mirror of my reality to show me the way out. The way to a new awareness.

Maybe on the other side, I can get another job. A job that's not just a job but means something to me. Or go to a college that teaches what I'm actually interested in. Or start a Youtube channel and talk about the weird stuff I love. And people will listen.

Maybe, one day, people I love will listen.

On our wedding day, Brent said to me, "I don't always understand you, but I understand that I love you."

It was true. That was our reality then. Maybe we were never perfect, but for a time, our quantum states were similar.

But realities degrade. They shift. They move like tides with time and the press of other gravities. It feels natural and inevitable. A cycle of life and death. And life after death.

Brent creates because he feels death beside him. But I also create. I create realities. And I don't create because I don't want to die, but because I want to live.

I close my eyes and step through the portal. It's like passing from winter into the smell of freshly cut grass.

I'm sorry, Brent. I'm sorry I waited so long to tell you goodbye. I do love you. That was real. Please find happiness now. We no longer have to pretend.

You and I, we're just not similar anymore.

#Eddie_and_June
Daniel Arthur Smith

I KNOW YOU'RE WONDERING how it is that a good girl like me, little ole June Hollis, ended up with a boy like Eddie Mayne, so I'll tell you, it's simpler than you'd think—it was fate. I know it sounds silly. I used to think that too. Anytime anyone would go on about how they'd met their soulmate just sounded dumb. Like it was meant to be—no two ways about it—that one soul was the only possible person for them. That's like saying that no matter what you do, your life is already decided for you, and that's ridiculous. At least, that's what I used to think. But meeting Eddie changed everything, because he and I were definitely meant to be.

When you think about it, the world couldn't work any other way. I mean, I'm no scientist or nothing, but I believe what I see with my own eyes. If you hold a ball in your hand, reach your arm straight out, then let it go, that ball's not going to float straight up or sideways—no sir, it's going to drop straight down. You can try to change it.

You can throw the ball as hard as you want and it may fly up for a while, but sooner or later, it's going to fall.

No matter how hard you try, you can't cheat fate.

All life is like that, from the day you're born. Whether you choose this or that, turn left instead of right, you'll always end up in the same place. Sometimes it only starts with a ball. Take the way I met Eddie. If Billy Clay wouldn't have been playing with that ball at lunch, Johnny G. wouldn't have knocked it out of his hand and into Jenna, and she wouldn't have spilled her smoothie onto my skirt. It was that ball that sent me to the ladies to clean my skirt and that's where I ran into Ingrid and Anna.

Now, Ingrid and Anna are school friends and all, I mean I've known them since kindergarten, but we don't normally hang out, and I'd have thought it was just by chance I ran into them—but it wasn't. They were telling me that Sally and Mara were hiding in the auditorium light booth with a bottle of wine that Sally stole from her mother, and that Sally was getting tipsy, and how it was funny, and if I didn't believe them, I should go see for myself—which I did.

It would have ended there, except Anna likes to post a lot to Instagram and she took a selfie with me, Ingrid, Sally, and Mara in the background, and clear as day, Sally had that bottle of Boones in her hand, and because Anna's mother follows her on Instagram, it was only a matter of a few short minutes after she posted that campus security was knocking on the door.

Now the way I see it, I was always meant to go with those girls to the light booth, because it was that selfie with the bottle of Boones that sealed it. Principal Bailor gave us detention for a week, which was bad enough, but on top of that we all had to go to one of those alcoholics anonymous meetings every week for the rest of the semester. The whole semester. I told Principal Bailor that it was unfair because I was just checking in on those girls and I didn't even drink so there was no way I have a drinking problem, and he said that if I was in my current situation, then I had a problem, and I had to go.

Now, I'd seen Eddie around once or twice I guess, but I didn't know him before that. He's from the northside across the river and I'd never had reason to go over there, and I'd never be caught dead near the way-back bleachers where he and his friends hid out. But because of Billy Clay's ball, and Jenna's smoothie, and Sally's mom's bottle of Boones, I found myself sitting across from him in the group circle—our AA meeting, it turned out, was just a student group led by Mister Benson, the school guidance counselor. Anyway, it was the first time I ever really paid any attention to him, and I noticed right off that he was—what's the word? Not just cute, or dreamy, but *striking*. Yes, that's it. He was striking, right off. He looked like he could be a model, like he was one of those boys from Netflix. He was wearing a jean jacket over a black tee, and kinda staring off out toward the window like he was somewhere else. I don't know why, but my tummy went all aflutter like it never has before, and wherever he was dreaming about, I wanted to be there with him, and I guess I was because I kinda heard Mister Benson say my name, but it didn't click until he said it a second or third time. That's when he caught my attention and that's when I caught Eddie's.

Now, that's the thing with fate, it doesn't just apply to you—there's plenty to go around. You see, Eddie was destined to meet me too and he'd be the first to say it. He and some of the other boys, Ronnie D. and a boy he calls Grubb, were caught with a bottle of Peppermint

Schnapps, except it was on the ground, and they said it wasn't theirs, but on account that it was under the way-back bleachers, and they were under the way-back bleachers, and they all smelled like peppermint, they were in the group too.

And, like I said, it was when Mister Benson had to say my name three times that Eddie's eyes dropped down and into mine and he shot me the sweetest smile that made me feel like we were thinking of the same thing, and that's how the rest of group went. I took my turn talking about my day and then Anna started talking about her mom, and the whole time, Eddie and me smiling at each other like we were in on the same joke.

After we were done, and everybody started to leave, Eddie sent his friends on without him so he could walk with me. Anytime before, if a boy did that, I'd have thought they were getting fresh and made an excuse to get rid of them, but I didn't do that with Eddie, because I just knew. I mean, I didn't know about fate yet, but I felt there was something special about him.

As he was walking me, we talked about all sorts of things and it turned out we had so much in common. I mean, who could imagine? We liked the same Netflix shows, and we liked the same songs. We talked about how neither of us thought it made much sense to have to do half the things they made us do in school, especially the after-school group, though we both agreed that right at that moment, since it had brought us together, we were happy about that. We talked so much, we kind of lost track of time and where we were going. Before I knew it, I looked up and we were downtown, outside Miller's Drug. I remembered I had to pick up some face cream for my mother and Eddie said he'd go in with me.

When we passed the magazines, I saw Cosmopolitan so I stopped and picked up a copy. He grabbed the one behind it and read, "Six steps to sexy hair," off the cover and, quick as a whistle, I said, "Number four will surprise you." And we both laughed. He asked me if the magazine was any good and I told him I liked the articles and the fashion, and I thought the quizzes were fun, but most of all I liked the idea of what happens in the city. I put the magazine back and we went to find my mom's face cream.

When we left the store, I told Eddie that I had to catch the bus and he asked if he could wait with me because it stops right there in front of Miller's. We talked a little more and when we saw the bus coming down the street, Eddie reached under his jean jacket, pulled out that copy of Cosmopolitan I was looking at, and held it toward me.

I didn't take it.

"You're naughty," I said. "Unless you're going to tell me that you had that magazine under your jacket this whole time."

He gave me a sly smile. "You wanted it," he said.

"I didn't want you to break the law."

"It's just a little thing. Big companies like that don't care." He walked over toward the corner trash. "But if you don't want it."

"No, you don't," I said and snatched it from him. "I don't want to be wasteful."

He gave me the magazine, then asked me for my phone.

"You don't have one?" I asked.

"Just give me yours," he said. "You'll see."

I handed him my phone and he fiddled with it. "There," he said. "I thought so."

"Thought what?" I asked.

He held it up in front of us. "Hold up your magazine and smile," he said. Then took a selfie of us with me holding the magazine.

The bus pulled up with a hiss of the breaks and the double door flew open, but Eddie was still fiddling with my phone. "C'mon," I said. "I gotta go."

"Okay," he said, handing me my phone. "I'll see you tomorrow."

"Maybe," I said. I should've been mad at him, but I wasn't. But I was already looking forward to it. All the way home, I was admiring that picture of the two of us and could barely sleep that night. He had added a hashtag with our names #Eddie_and_June.

When I arrived at school the next day, Eddie and Grubb were out in the front, leaning on the side of a big silver SUV. I don't know much about cars so I couldn't tell you the name, but it wasn't one of those mini-vans; it was something sporty with a fancy logo.

"Is that your car?" I asked him.

"It's my uncle's," he said. "He let me borrow it. I thought you might like to go for a ride into the city."

"When? After school?"

"I was thinking right now."

"I can't miss school."

"The thing is," he said, "is that I only have it for the day. If we want to go, we should go now."

"My Mom is going to get a call."

"Just text her. She'll understand."

That was another point where things should've just stopped. I mean, slam on the breaks, right there in front of the school. And I did think about it for a second, especially the idea that my mother would *understand*. But Eddie, he can turn his eyes into saucers and once his eyes said please, the decision was made. I pulled out my phone, sent a text to my mother saying not to worry, then yelled, "Shotgun!" and ran to the passenger side.

"Hold on," he said. "You'll have to drive."

"Why can't you?"

"I don't have my license."

"You don't have your license? Why's that?"

"There was an issue."

"Then how'd you get here?"

"Grubb drove. You have yours though, right?"

"Sure," I said. I shrugged my shoulders and headed to the driver's side. "If you feel safe with me behind the wheel, I'm happy to drive."

Eddie waved off his buddy Grubb. "I have no issue putting my life in your hands." Then he hopped in.

"This is nice," I said. The inside of the car was as fancy as the logo with dark polished wood trimming the doors and dash.

"With all these shiny buttons and digital screens, it looks like the controls to a rocket ship," I said, adjusting the mirror. "Now, where is the key?"

"Here it is," said Eddie. He fished the keychain from the console cupholder and dangled it in front of me. I reached for them and he snagged them away.

"Hey," I said.

"You don't need them," he said. "Watch this. Push down on the brakes and," he pushed a button in the dash behind the steering wheel. And just like that, the car started. I'd like to say that I'm not that easily impressed, but I'd never seen that before. And that wasn't all; the stereo had a satellite radio with a jillion stations and there were speakers everywhere. Eddie let me play whatever I liked because it was what he liked too, which was good because it was a long drive to the city. But saying that, it didn't seem long. After listening to music for a while, we got to talking again. That's when he asked me what I thought about fate, and I told him didn't, because up until then, I really hadn't. Then he told me about the ball having to fall and how it was our destiny to meet each other because fate wanted us to be together, and the way he explained it, it all made perfect sense to me.

We were in the city by lunch and had such a wonderful time visiting places and taking pictures, tagging them all #Eddie_and_June. We went to the art museum, shared some potato chips and a banana in the park, and even went into a Tiffany's. I guess you'd say that's where things took a turn. Eddie said he wanted to go in because he'd never been and had heard the name so many times. I wasn't about to disagree because we were having such a great time and, after all, it was Tiffany's.

Right when we walked in, I could tell Eddie was trying to make himself invisible.

"You okay?" I asked him.

"It's all the rich people. They make me nervous."

"You don't know they're rich," I said.

But then he said, "It's the middle of the day and instead of being at their jobs, they're shopping in a jewelry store."

I said, "Maybe they all work the night shift," and we both had a chuckle.

He was right, though; there were a lot of people in there, especially for a weekday, and who else but rich people could afford to spend their time like that? You see, Eddie's insightful like that. Anyway, by that time, it already felt natural to wrap my arm around his and lead him past the display cases to make him feel a bit better. It worked because lickety split, we were joking again. Joking a little about how some of the people were dressed, and a little about some of the rings and necklaces and stuff. There was this bracelet that caught my eye, and I guess I slowed because Eddie caught on right away and he asked one of the sales people if we could have a look. She was a pretty woman who looked more like she was dressed for a party than a jewelry store, and she was really nice. It kind of surprised me how pleasant she was, particularly because it seemed she didn't pay it no mind that we were teenagers. I guess in her day to day, it was completely normal for kids to come off the street to buy stuff. She set a black velvety cloth on the glass, then unlocked the display case, pulled out the tray of bracelets, and placed it on top. There were five dainty chains on the tray, each a different color and polished to a high sheen. I pointed to the one I liked, and she fastened it around my wrist. "That's my favorite," she said, "and it looks beautiful on you. I love rose gold."

"I do too," I said but I never knew that until right then.

"How much is it?" I asked.

"Six hundred," she said as she unfastened it. "Would you like me to wrap it?"

"We'll think about it," I said, and she smiled back.

She unlocked the display case to put the tray back, then I said, "Oh. I want to take a picture."

She stepped back while I took another selfie. Then another customer who couldn't wait, leaned across the glass at the far end of the counter and called her over, so she smiled and stepped away to help the woman. I tagged our Tiffany's picture #Eddie_and_June like all of the others. It was a good picture. I scrolled through my feed and was pleasantly surprised by what I saw. "Would you look at that," I said to Eddie, showing him my screen. "We have so many likes. It's phenomenal."

He took my phone from me to get a better look. "That's awesome," he said. Then quickly handed the phone back. "Hey. You know what? It's getting late. We have to go."

"Oh. Okay," I said, but he already had a hold of my arm and was shuffling me out. He pushed us past the crowd of people at the entrance and out the huge revolving glass door and onto the sidewalk.

"All right," he said. "Let's get back to the car." Then pulled me to the corner. As we were waiting for the light, he took my hand in his, reached into his pocket and, you'd never guess it, he pulled out that rose gold bracelet and slipped it into my palm. "Eddie! What did you do?"

"I got it for you, silly."

"You shouldn't have done that."

"You like it, don't you?"

"Well, yes. But—"

"Hey, you!" a man yelled from behind us. "Hold it right there."

I spun back to see a huge bald man in a black suit double stepping toward us. With a jerk, Eddie pulled me into traffic. As I was turning, I heard a horn and a squeal of breaks—right in front of me was a yellow taxi. I would have frozen right there and then, but Eddie yelled, "Run, June, run!" He was still pulling at my arm and it seemed like I was in front of that car for an eternity, but it must not have been because before I even knew what was happening, I was planting one foot in front of the other, flying down the avenue.

We cut across the street, right through traffic, and into the middle of a crowd of tourists. I heard more horns, tires squealing, and yelling behind me, but I didn't look back. Eddie was leading the way. We rounded a corner and he pulled me into a deli and behind a stand of potato chips. My heart was racing so fast. It was like being on a roller coaster. He peeked around the side and he must have seen the security man go by, because just as quick as we'd darted off before, he said, "Let's go," and towed me out the door and down the stairs to the train.

When we got to the platform, a train was pulling up, so he jumped the turnstile then lifted me right over like I was a feather. I don't even remember the last few steps because I was laughing out loud. I mean, it's silly for me to think about now, but I couldn't control myself. I must have been hysterical because I was literally laughing out loud. He must've pulled me into the train car because my next thought was the train starting to move and the both of us out of breath and laughing. I tell you, it was painful; my chest felt like it was likely to explode.

W caught our breath at the same time and stopped laughing, and you know what? That's when Eddie and I had our first kiss.

I took a selfie right there in the train, so we'd remember.

The train turned us around a little bit, and I have to admit that once we were back on the street, I kept looking over my shoulder, but we made it back to where we parked the car without any more problems and then we were on our way. Once we were outside the city, I remembered the bracelet. I pulled that little rose gold chain from my pocket and let it dangle in front of me. The rose gold was even prettier in the SUV then it had been in the store. My mind raced back through the events of the day and how it was that I had such a beautiful piece of jewelry and I almost couldn't believe it. Again, I should have been mad, but that wasn't at all what I was feeling. Up to that point in my life, I never felt so alive. So I slipped it around my wrist and had Eddie fasten the latch.

That's when Eddie started talking about destiny again. "That chain was meant for you," he said. "From the moment it was made, it was just a matter of time before you found each other."

I about melted right there because by that time, I'd already become a true believer. Everything with Eddie just felt so right. We talked some more and when a song came on the radio that we loved, we'd turn it up and sing along, one song after another. It was like Car Karaoke with all of our favorite songs.

After a while, we saw a sign for the next rest stop. We were both starting to get hungry and they had a Chick-fil-A. Besides, we had to fill up the car, so it all worked out.

It was funny, because I was fine up until we hit that exit ramp, but right then I realized with all the excitement, I hadn't been to the ladies. So I asked Eddie if we could just park and fill up after and he said that was fine.

When I came out, he was still waiting in line, so joined him at the counter. He was frustrated because it was taking a little while, but when we finally did get our food, we found a seat over by the window, away from everybody else, and it was romantic in a Chick-fil-A sort of way. I was in the middle of my fries and getting lost in Eddie's eyes when a state police cruiser stole my attention. Eddie didn't pay it no mind, but I saw it slow down then stop right behind the SUV.

"Eddie," I said. "They've stopped behind our car."

Now, Eddie couldn't see them because the car was parked behind where he was sitting, but I could see what was happening clear as day over his right shoulder.

"They have to park somewhere," he said.

I sunk down in my seat a bit. "Yes. That's true, they have to park somewhere. But now one of them has gotten out and is peeking through the car windows."

"Relax. Just finish eating."

"Relax? What are we going to do? How they'd know that's our car."

"You didn't leave anything in the car did you?"

"No. Why?"

Eddie sighed. "They're not looking for us. They're looking for the car."

"What do you mean?"

"I thought we had plenty of time to get it back to the garage."

"Garage? Eddie, I thought you said your uncle let you borrow it."

"Well, that wasn't exactly the case."

"You mean he doesn't know you have it?"

"I mean, it's not my uncle's car. It's a car Grubb and I borrowed from the overnight parking garage. We do it all the time. As long as we have it back by morning, nobody knows the difference."

"I see."

"They don't know who drove it in here. Just act natural. When they're finished, I'll find us another way out of here."

So that's what I did. I kept at my french fries, with one eye on the state police officer. He was writing things down on a little pad, like the license plate and I don't know what else. I watched him as he went back over to his police car to check with his partner. Then I watched him walk up to the rest area door.

"Eddie," I said again. "He's coming in here."

Eddie didn't even look back over his shoulder. He was rock solid calm. "Don't panic," he said. "I told you. He doesn't know it's us." Then he went back to his chicken sandwich. The whole time the officer was back by the door, scanning the place.

"He certainly looks like he's looking for someone."

Eddie shirked it away, but he was chewing a lot slower. I could tell his wheels were spinning.

"Eddie," I said. "He's going over to the counter aaand—"

"Maybe he wants a donut." Eddie grinned.

"Well," I said. "He's asking the Chick-fil-A guy something."

"And?"

"The Chick-fil-A guy is shaking his head like he doesn't have an answer."

Eddie took the last bite of his sandwich, smiled, then said, "Maybe you should take those fries to go." We calmly stood up and walked toward the door—right past that officer. The policeman smiled at me the way all men smile at a young lady, polite like, and that gave me an idea. I smiled back—a big full smile—then asked him if he'd mind if we took a picture with him. He hesitated for split second, then he said, "Sure."

So Eddie and I spun around and snapped another #Eddie_and_June. Eddie kept a happy look on his face, but he was squeezing my hand real tight, and as soon as we said thank you, he had me out the door and out toward the parking lot to get us as far away from the SUV and police cruiser as he could.

Any joy I got out of seeing Eddie squirm disappeared once we were clear of the rest stop and I punched him in the arm to let him know. "Are you crazy?" I asked. "You know what kind of trouble you could've gotten us into?"

"It shouldn't have been that big of deal," he said. "Grubb and I borrow cars from the garage all the time. People bring them in when they're going on business trips and stuff like that. That car wasn't even supposed to be picked up until Friday."

I slapped him in the arm again. "It *is* Friday!"

"No, it's…Oh, I guess you're right."

He was so cute. I couldn't stay mad. I did tell him, though, that he better have a plan to get us out of there or else. So, he got on his phone and called his friend Grubb to come pick us up. I heard him leave a voicemail, but it didn't sound good. After he hung up, he told me that Grubb didn't answer and probably wouldn't call back until the morning. Then we saw the red flashing lights of another cruiser rolling up from the highway to join the first.

Eddie bit his lip and began scanning the lot for I don't know what. But then he landed on something. "We can't go back the way we came," said Eddie. He gestured to the far side of the parking lot and a tall Motel 6 sign towering above the trees. "I still have some money left. We could go over there and get a room 'til morning."

"Are you sure there isn't someone else we can call?"

"We can call your mother."

"Hah, hah," I said. "Are you kidding me? She'd skin me alive."

"Well, we could. Or we could go to the motel and just get some rest until morning."

I didn't think it was a very good idea to stay the night with a boy on what was essentially our first date, but then again, I wasn't too happy about having found out how he had *borrowed* that car or that calling my mother really was our only other option apart from sitting outside until morning. "I see your point. All right, we can stay for the night. But you have to promise to be a gentleman."

"Of course. But you're going to have tell your mother something. She'll be worried."

I rolled my eyes and started walking toward the Motel 6. "I'm not going to tell her anything," I said. "It's Friday, so I'll just text that I'm staying out with friends."

The creepy old man at the desk gave me the oddest smile when we asked for two beds but when Eddie put his cash on the desk, he gave us two key cards and sent us up to our room, which by the way, wasn't as bad as I feared. I don't know what I thought a cheap motel room would be like; I suppose I imagined a real dump. But the room was fine—just bland.

Eddie was a gentleman. I suppose I would have been okay if he kissed me again. But he climbed up onto one of the beds and said, "You go ahead and take a shower. I'll go after you." Then he grabbed the remote and put on the TV.

When I was done, I put on one of the robes I found hanging in the closet. They weren't the big fluffy kind, but since I didn't have anything else to wear, I was quite satisfied because, as far as I was concerned, it was a bonus just to have them in a Motel 6. I came out to tell Eddie he could take his turn, but he was already asleep. He was so cute. I turned off the TV, grabbed my phone, then snuggled up against him to take another #Eddie_and_June. Right before I snapped the picture, he slid his arm over my shoulder and cuddled back. Talk about a million shivers, I don't know if I ever felt so good. Now, I planned to sleep in the other bed, I did, but I was so tired—and comfortable—I didn't see any harm in resting my eyes for just minute, but I must've passed right out because the next thing I know, Eddie was standing above me, gently shoving my shoulder, and whispering, "Wake up, wake up." And when I did, I wasn't exactly sure where I was or how much time had passed. The room was real dark except for the sliver of red and blue flashing light coming through the slit between the curtains.

Eddie's was talking a little fast. "It's the police," he said. "They've been circling the motel for the last ten minutes. You have to get dressed."

My brain was a bit foggy and it took me a second to take it in. I was remembering where we were and why, which didn't settle well right then, but I said, "Okay." Then I made my way to the bathroom and put my clothes on. I came back out and Eddie was peeking out the curtains.

"You think they're looking for us?" I asked.

"I don't know for sure…But yes."

I went over next to Eddie to see the cruiser pass by again. Sure enough, the car had just rounded the corner of the lot and was slowly driving our way.

In a whisper, I asked Eddie, "How do you think they found us?"

"Maybe that old coot at the desk."

That sounded right to me. That smelly old man would have given us up in a second ,but... "Wouldn't they just have come right to the door then?"

"Yeah," said Eddie. "It's a mystery."

We backed away from the window as the cruiser passed directly below. Then, as if on cue, we heard a loud buzzing noise from the bedside table. It was my phone and it was making that vibrating sound it does when someone calls but the ringer's off. The screen was facedown, so I picked it up to see who was calling.

"Who is it?" asked Eddie.

"The screen says no caller ID."

"Who'd be calling you this late?"

Then we both looked at each other with the same realization.

"June," said Eddie. "That's how they're tracking us."

I tossed the phone onto the bed.

Eddie took a step back. "You have to shut it off."

"No. You shut it off," I said. "I'm not going near it."

Eddie scrunched his face, walked over to the bed, and picked it up, but before he could turn it off, I stopped him. "Wait," I said. "If they're tracking the signal, and you turn it off, they'll know that we're on to them. Leave it be, and let's get as far away from here as we can."

"Right," said Eddie. He gently set the phone down on the bed. "Let's get going." He slipped on his jacket then went back over to the curtain. "You ready?"

With however much sleep I'd had and a fresh rush of adrenalin, I was wide awake. "Yes," I said, putting my hand on the door handle. "Let's go."

"Wait a sec," he said. Still peeking out. "They're rounding the corner. All right, we're clear, but we gotta move."

I eased the door open, then remembered. "Leave your phone too," I said.

"But they didn't try to call me."

"Not yet. Leave it and let's go."

"I'm not going to make it easy for them," he said as he stepped close to me. "There's a pick-up truck down there. I'll toss it in the back."

"I love how you think," I said. And threw my arms around him and we squeezed each other tight. Then

Eddie took my hand and the two of us slipped out into the night.

The sky was overcast so it was too dark for anyone to see us as we made our way across the parking lot. But we wanted to be safe, so we ducked behind a car to stay hidden in the shadows.

From where we crouched, we could easily see who was coming and going, to and from the pumps, and it didn't take long before Eddie saw someone leave their car running. He tugged my sleeve and we raced toward it. It was an older car, one of those Jeeps that's shaped like two boxes put together, and when we got close and he pointed through the window, I realized why he chose it. Not only was the car running, but the key was in the ignition. Eddie was smart that way—an old car would mean a real metal key rather that an electric one like the one in the SUV. Eddie opened the driver's door and climbed in, crawling all the way to the passenger side. I slipped in behind him.

I whispered, "I don't think it matters anymore if you have a license."

He said, "I just feel better if you're driving. I'm a bit edgy."

I wasn't going to argue with him because we didn't have time to spare. The driver could be walking back out any second. Lucky for me it was an automatic, because I'd never learned to drive a stick. I threw the car into drive and pulled out of that rest stop nice and easy, like it was my own car, then drove back onto the highway. The thing is, of course, it wasn't my car. If you would've told me that morning that I'd be stealing a car, I would've called you crazy. I certainly wasn't happy about it. But in that one day, the world had changed, because without even realizing it, I'd already been driving a stolen car all day.

Funny thing is, it just seemed natural to take that car. Like it was meant to be. And I was calm as a cucumber. At least, I was calm at first. Okay, I guess maybe more focused than calm, but you see, that didn't last long. A mile down the road, I noticed that my heart was pounding a million beats per minute and Eddie and I, we were both checking the mirrors for any signs of flashing lights. Fortunately, there weren't any.

I drove a ways like that, both my hands white knuckled from squeezing the wheel, my eyes darting mirror to mirror every five seconds, and neither of us had a word to say to each other. Then Eddie turned on the radio. It wasn't a satellite radio like the SUV but an old time FM stereo. Eddie dialed through to find a music station and wouldn't you know it, the first song he found was one of my favorites, and right then, a weight was lifted. Funny how much a song can change everything, I mean in that split second. Not just the music itself, but the words, like when you sing along, and those words are applying to you. It was fate at work again, because those words were just about as spot on as any could be—a full tank, on the run—and it wasn't lost on Eddie either. By the end of the song, we were singing at the top of our lungs. It was all very exciting.

And I think it was right then and there we decided that just like the song, we weren't going back; it was clear as day that we were going to run.

There was no reason to go back anyway, because no one was going to believe our side of the story, that Eddie just meant to borrow the SUV and planned to return it before anyone was the wiser. And certainly, there was no way to explain away the car we had now. No. We'd be in deep trouble; they'd lock us up and throw away the key. Eddie, for sure, and that would be the end of that; no more Eddie and no more us. We wouldn't be able to see each other again, we wouldn't be allowed—and I was just getting used to the idea of us being together.

"Where to next?" I asked.

"Well," said Eddie, "the tank is full. We can go anywhere."

"I'm out of money."

"Me too, I think." He dug through his jeans and pulled out a crumpled wad of bills from each pocket. He separated them and counted. "Eight dollars," he said. "I spent everything else on the room. But..." he climbed up on the seat and turned toward the back. "When we got in, I saw a bunch of camping stuff back here." Then he began rifling through the contents of the backseat.

"Anything good back there?" I asked.

"I think we hit the lottery. The guy must be a hiker. There's two backpacks, a tent...two sleeping bags...some other gear." He flicked a light on and off. "An electric lantern, some flashlights."

"Any food?"

"Um," he said. "Just a second..." He handed me a bottle of water.

"Thanks," I said.

"There's a whole case back here." He spun back around into his seat with his hands full. "Between the two-pack, I found four power bars and some trail mix. You want one?"

"Wow. What a score," I said. "I'll have one later. I'm not really hungry now."

"Me either," he said.

"You didn't answer me. Where to next?"

"Just drive, I guess," said Eddie. "And we'll see where the fates take us."

And that's just what I did.

We weren't tired. We talked, and sang, and talked. There were a few more moments of liberation. My tummy did a flip when we passed our exit, and a few more songs came on the radio that justified our plan—a plan that was really no plan at all, just to drive.

The time flew by and before I knew it, the low fuel light came on. Eddie said we'd have to do what he called a Pump and Run. He said we'd just pump the gas and go. But when we stopped at the pump, we realized that wouldn't work because you had to pre-pay or use a credit card and we only had that eight dollars between the two of us and the emergency credit card my mother gave me. Now, I could have used that emergency card, but I'd seen enough TV and movies to know that as soon as I did, the police would know exactly where we were at, just like with the phones.

So we ended up doing the same thing we did the first time. We parked and waited for someone to pump and leave their car—then we ran over and borrowed it. That next one was easy, so was the next and the next, and that just became the thing we did.

We got lucky again and again. One car had a wad of cash on the console, another was full of groceries. They even had Twinkies and Diet Coke. All right, so I guess we weren't borrowing the food or money, but we never did anything more than put a few miles on the cars. We'd moved off the main roads and it got so that we'd drive for a while then find a place to park and rest, and it wasn't too long that we'd put a lot of distance between us and where we started. And Eddie and I, we were getting to know each other a lot better, if you know what I mean. He's a real good kisser.

Everything was going as swell as it could go for two fugitives. Then things became real interesting. We stretched everything out as far as we could but the groceries we found early on didn't last long and we were on a tight budget with the money we'd found. So to stay fed, we developed a routine. We got into the habit of stopping at those mini-marts, the ones with the gas stations. I mean, just about every gas station has a mini-mart, but we liked this one chain that was bigger because they had coolers with real food, like salads, sandwiches, milk, and orange juice. The chain was called Stop-N-Buy, or Stop-N-Shop, or Stop-N-Go. I really don't remember. Eddie called the place a Stop-N-Rob, that's what sticks in my mind and that's pretty much what we did whenever we saw one. Eddie would go in first and then I'd follow a minute later so it didn't look like we were together. I'd take one of those backpacks that we got with the first car into the store, open the zipper, and walk around with it partly open by my side so that when Eddie would pass me at the end of the aisle and out of sight, he could drop stuff into it, all nonchalant like. Then we'd go up to the counter separately and buy something small like a candy bar. That works a lot better than you'd think, because the clerks usually don't watch you too well.

Well, we were at one of those Stop-n-Robs when I realized this girl is holding up her phone and recording me and Eddie. And she wasn't all that discrete about it, she was just standing at the aisle with a big smile on her face, pointing that phone right at us. I could maybe understand it if she'd seen Eddie drop something into the bag, but he hadn't. I tried to ignore her, thinking maybe

Daniel Arthur Smith

she was mental, and moved over to the next aisle—but she just followed, so I finally asked, "Can I help you?"

The girl lowered her phone. She still had a big smile, but she didn't say anything, just kept smiling, and her cheeks got all rosie, like she was embarrassed.

I walked toward her, and she took half a step back, so I asked, "Are you okay?" about sure by this time that she indeed was mental.

She spoke up and said, "I'm sorry." Then added, "I can't believe it's you."

That caught me off guard. *Believe it's me?* I thought. So I asked her, "And just who do you think I am?"

"You're June," she said. "Hashtag Eddie and June."

I admit, I was dumbfounded. "How'd you know that?"

She didn't hesitate. She raised her phone to show me the screen and said, "You're famous."

"You mean," I asked, "everyone is following my Instagram feed?"

"More than that," she said. "Have you searched your hashtag?"

"No," I said. "I don't even have my phone anymore." I held out my hand. "Let me see yours."

She handed me her phone and I went to my account. "Oh my mother," I said when I saw my feed. "That can't be right. It says I have millions of likes."

"That post has thirty million," said the girl. "That's four million more than the old record, but that's nothing, let me show you the hashtag—" she reached for the phone, but this time I was the one to take a step back and said, "I know how to do it."

I tapped the #Eddie_and_June tag from my feed, but I wasn't prepared for what I saw. "Eddie," I said. "I don't believe this."

60

Having spoken to me, the girl wasn't too timid anymore, she stepped over next to me all happy to help. "Eddie and June has been trending for days," she said, then swiped the feed while I held the phone. I didn't see any pictures from my feed, but there were plenty from the security camera at Tiffany's, the city sidewalk, the Chick-fil-A, the gas stations, a bunch of the other Stop-N-Robs—all with the Eddie_and_June hash tag—and that wasn't all. There were so many pictures from strangers rooting us on that had the hashtag too. The girl kept swiping and the pictures kept coming—picture after picture.

By this time, Eddie was looking over my other shoulder. "Would you look at that," he said.

"I told you," said the girl. "You're famous." Then she yelled behind her, "Billy. It is her."

Apparently, Billy was the clerk's name and, as I was in a bit of shock with all of this new information, I didn't even realize that he was watching us. "I thought that was you," he said in the friendliest way. "Eddie and June. You're more famous than the Kardashians."

"Show her the TV," said the girl. "She doesn't know."

"All right," said Billy. "Come over here and I'll show you."

We should have marched out the door right then and there, but curiosity had the better of us, so we went over to the counter. Billy the clerk changed the channel on the tv to the news and there we were—the main story. Wolf Blitzer was talking to a state trooper while some of the same pictures from the feed showed in the corner, and all the while the ticker at the bottom said we were outlaws being pursued not only by police, but because we'd crossed state lines, the FBI were after us too.

"Oh my mother," I said again. I handed the girl back her phone. "I'm sorry. It was nice to meet you, but I think we better go."

"Can we get a selfie first?" asked the girl.

Eddie and I looked at each other surprised. "You can't deny the public," he said.

So we posed for a selfie with Billy and the girl, then tagged it for them #Eddie_and_June.

"And you can take whatever you want," added Billy. "We're on your side."

"Excuse me?" I said.

"Yeah. We don't mind. Here. These are the candy bars you like. Right?" He slid a full box across the counter. "Take 'em all. And whatever you want from the cooler."

Eddie and I looked at each other again, shrugged, then went over to the food counter to fill up with smoothies, burgers, and hot dogs—all the stuff we usually had to stay away from.

And that's how that became a thing. When word got out that we were friendly, people were asking us left and right to take a selfie with them, and we would. It got to be that we didn't have to steal no more. I mean, we were suspicious at first, but somehow people had this idea that we were the good guys, on the run, and it didn't matter what our reasons were, they just wanted to help us. We had become celebrities, famous for being famous, famous for being Eddie and June. All we had to do was show up, and anything was ours for the taking. They even let us fill the tank, so we didn't have to switch cars so often anymore, and if we did have to switch there were people volunteering theirs, telling us they'd wait a few days or a week to report it.

There was never any danger, not from regular people anyway. We started to hear about ourselves on the radio, how the FBI was tracking us by the location ID in the pictures. A couple times, clerks had scanners and they'd let us know which direction to go to avoid trouble. It was like the whole country was on our side.

I mean, it wasn't all that. We were still eating junk food and sleeping out under the stars. But we had each other, and we were young and in love. It was fate and there's nothing could be done about that.

But you see, that's a thing too. Fate. Because it ain't all good things that are meant to be, and no matter how hard you try, you can't cheat fate. You just can't, and it presents itself when you least expect it—like when I met Eddie—you won't know where or when it'll hit. Who would've guessed we'd be in a small-town drug store, taking a selfie with the cashier, when fate would come knocking again. It's funny really, with all the state troopers and the FBI and who knows who else all searching the country for us, but it was that young deputy who just happened to walk in while we were posing. And just like everybody else, he recognized us, but he didn't see things the way everyone else had. He certainly didn't think we were the good guys. He was afraid; and he drew his gun, and yelled, "Hold it right there!"

I said to him, "You don't need to wave a gun like that. We'll be on our way."

But the deputy, he wasn't having it. He kept that gun pointed right at us.

Eddie whispered in my ear that he didn't think the deputy would shoot and that we should just slowly walk out. But the deputy wasn't having that either. Eddie was half right. The deputy didn't shoot, but he did grab Eddie by his jean jacket, and Eddie squirmed to get free, and Eddie's jacket was over his head, and the two were wrestling around, and it looked pretty silly—but then that gun went off and shot me.

The nurse said the doctors fixed me right up. I lost some blood, but the bullet went in and out which she said was a good thing, so I suppose it's true. But that's a world of pain, let me tell you. It was too much, and I passed out, but not before I saw Eddie get away.

Of course, then I did pass out and woke up here and met you nice folks, and that's about the whole story.

Mrs. Hollis ran her fingers through her frazzled, graying hair and took a deep breath. She was dressed well, a professional, and still appeared quite youthful despite the deep stress lines beneath the veil of her smile and the dark rings barely hidden beneath her freshly applied makeup. Her daughter June was in a hospital bed on the other side of the door, and though Mrs. Hollis didn't really understand how that came to be, when the uniformed officer guarding the door asked her if she was ready, she put on a brave face and replied as cheerfully as she could, "As I'll ever be." The officer tapped a code into the security keypad on the wall. There was a loud buzz, and the hospital room door clicked open.

There were two people standing on the far side of the bed, a man and a woman, both in suits. Mrs. Hollis guessed they were police. There had been a parade of detectives.

June was already smiling, but her face lit up when Mrs. Hollis entered the room. "Mother," she said. "I'm glad you're back. This man is Detective Meyer and she's Doctor Rosario."

Half right, thought Mrs. Hollis.

"Hello, Detective and Doctor…"

"Rosario," she said.

"Are you one of my daughter's doctors?"

"I'm the department psychiatrist. It's standard for me to check in with gun shot victims. June was just telling us a story about fate and such."

Mrs. Hollis' eyes sank. *Two detectives.* "Oh," she said, then pushed another smile forward. "I apologize for interrupting." She held up a bag of chocolate chips and a chocolate milk. "I've brought June a snack. I thought she might be hungry."

Detective Meyer gave Mrs. Hollis a sympathetic smile. "That's okay," he said. "Doctor Rosario and I were just leaving."

"I'm glad you brought me something to nibble on," said June. "But you'll have to feed me. For whatever reason, they seem to be afraid I'll fall out of bed." She shifted her wrists out from under the crumpled blanket. Each was bound with a five-inch-wide cushioned restraint strap.

Through the two-way mirror, the detective and psychiatrist observed June happily chatting with her mother as the woman fed her daughter pieces of chocolate chip cookie. Meyer scratched his chin. "That mumbo jumbo about fate was getting pretty thick. I mean, I get it, destiny and all that. But wow."

"I think it's kind of romantic," said Rosario. "I mean, every girl wants to find the right one. Why not have fate deliver him? And if he's a bad boy, all the better. Girls like this love bad boys and she found one who is definitely trouble."

"You didn't see the news coverage?"

"Honestly, we don't watch much television. I think I heard a few reports on the radio, but I wasn't really paying attention."

"And you haven't seen the Instagram feed?"

Rosario shook her head. "No. Should I?"

Meyer pulled a small digital pad from his pocket, tapped the screen a few times, then handed it to Rosario. "We've left the account open. Don't know how easily we could shut it down anyway. If she wasn't a celebrity before, she is now."

"The world we live in," said Rosario. "Famous for being famous." She began to swipe through the feed, and as she did her eyes widened. "They're all like this?"

Meyer nodded. "Every one."

"All these pictures in her feed, they're just…her. There's no sign of a boy. Every picture is just June by herself with the hashtag Eddie_and_June."

"That's because there is no Eddie."

Rosario shook her head. "She sounded so credible. What about that car? The story about the garage? The people she talked to at the mini-marts?"

"A parent left the car running in front of the school. They reported it stolen but it wasn't spotted until that evening at the rest stop," said Meyer. "The other witnesses thought Eddie and June was just a cool tag or had some other meaning. They never saw a boy in a jean jacket." Meyer set a fixed gaze onto June. She was talking to her mother—laughing. "You know, she may be the next Meryl Streep, but if I didn't know any better, I'd say that she really believes everything she just told us and believes that she spent all that time on the road with Eddie. I think she sees him no differently than you see me."

"She believes it, all right," said Rosario. "You see the way her eyes dart toward the door. She's expecting him to walk in any minute. She's lost all touch with reality. You're looking at a girl in love."

ABOUT THE AUTHORS

Hunter C. Eden is a Denver-based essayist and dark fantasy writer whose work has appeared in **Weird Tales**, **City Slab**, and **Ravenous Monster Horror Webzine**.

D.K. Cassidy is a USA Today bestselling author. She scribbles daily in various genres including Science Fiction, Magical Realism, & Urban Gothic. Her goal? Messing with your mind by transforming the voices in her head into odd stories.

She lives in the Pacific Northwest with her greatest fans: her husband Mark, twin sons Aidan and Jared, and four cats. When not writing, she loves to travel, run, knit, use the Oxford comma, and of course read!

David Alan Jones is a veteran of the US Air Force where he served as an Arabic linguist. He is also a martial artist, a husband, and a father of three. David writes novels that draw upon his experiences in intel and martial arts combined with his love of all things literary. An eclectic reader, David counts Anne Tyler, Stephen King, Lois McMaster Bujold, Robert J. Sawyer, J.K. Rowling and many others among his favorite, and most influential, authors.

Holly Heisey is an author, illustrator, and designer with a love of spaceships and a tendency to quote Monty Python. They've had stories in **Intergalactic Medicine Show**, **The Doomsday Chronicles**, **Clockwork Phoenix 5**, and **Transcendent: The Year's Best Transgender Speculative Fiction** volumes one and two, as well as translated into German and Estonian. Holly lives in Arizona with Larry, their pet cactus, who doesn't bite. They're currently at work on a space opera epic, and you can find them online at hollyheisey.com.

Jessica West (a.k.a. West1Jess) is currently pursuing a state of self-induced psychosis, also known as writing. In the past, she has worked for Wal-Mart, a lawyer, and a bank. Now if she could just get a couple years experience with the IRS and the NSA, world domination is in the bag.

Jess lives in Acadiana with three daughters still young enough to think she's cool and a husband who knows better but likes her anyway.

For news and updates visit west1jess.com

Daniel Arthur Smith is a USA Today bestselling author. His titles include *Spectral Shift*, *Hugh Howey Lives*, *The Cathari Treasure*, *The Somali Deception*, and a few other novels and short stories. He also curates the phenomenal short fiction series *Tales from the Canyons of the Damned* and *Frontiers of Speculative Fiction*.

He was raised in Michigan and graduated from Western Michigan University where he studied philosophy, with focus on cognitive science, meta-physics, and comparative religion. He began his career as a bartender, barista, poetry house proprietor, teacher, and then became a technologist and futurist for the Fortune 100 across the Americas and Europe.

Daniel has traveled to over 300 cities in 22 countries, residing in Los Angeles, Kalamazoo, Prague, Crete, and now writes in Manhattan where he lives with his wife and young sons.

For news and updates visit danielarthursmith.com

www.ingramcontent.com/pod-product-compliance
Lightning Source LLC
Chambersburg PA
CBHW020550130626
46552CB00007B/2844